WINTER
Wishes

Illustrated by Alison Edgson

STRIPES PUBLISHING
An imprint of Magi Publications
1 The Coda Centre, 189 Munster Road, London SW6 6AW

A paperback original
First published in Great Britain in 2011

This collection copyright © Stripes Publishing, 2011
Stories copyright © Caroline Juskus, Guy Bass, Michael Broad,
Caroline Pitcher, Elizabeth Baguley, Karen Wallace, Malachy Doyle,
Penny Dolan, Narinder Dhami, Holly Webb, 2011
Illustrations copyright © Alison Edgson, 2011

The right of Alison Edgson to be identified as the
illustrator of this work has been asserted by her in accordance
with the Copyright, Designs and Patents Act, 1988.

ISBN: 978-1-84715-201-5

A CIP catalogue record for this book is available from the British Library.

Printed and bound in the UK.

2 4 6 8 10 9 7 5 3 1

CONTENTS

THE PENGUIN PARADE

Caroline Juskus

Pip the little penguin hopped up and down, flapping his tiny, feathery flippers. He was bursting with excitement, for in two days' time, on Christmas morning, he and his big sister, Toots, were going to march in the Penguin Parade.

"The youngest penguins march at the front," explained Toots, "and if we march nicely, children bring us buckets of shiny, silvery, sparkly presents."

"Ooh!" said Pip. "What sort of shiny, silvery, sparkly presents?"

"It's a surprise," said Mum.

"Humph," said Pip. "Do you know, Toots?"

Toots giggled. "Of course I do. I'm older than you."

"That's not fair," said Pip. "Please tell me."

Mum shook her head. "It's tradition," she said. "Every young penguin gets a shiny surprise for their first Penguin Parade."

But Pip didn't want a surprise. He wanted to know NOW!

"Go and practise your marching," said Mum, tickling Pip under his chin. "You'll need to keep up with the other penguins, and lots of them are bigger than you."

Pip swung his flippers and jiggled his head.

"Don't forget to move your legs as well!" Toots laughed.

"I know that!" said Pip, waddling off. But secretly he had quite forgotten. He was too busy thinking about his shiny surprise.

Toots followed him. "Try and move your feet like me," she said.

Pip hopped in the air and shuffled his feet, but they tangled together and he toppled, beak first, into the crisp white snow.

"Silly Pip!" Toots chuckled. "Not so fast."

Pip shook the snow off his fluffy feathers and carefully placed one foot in front of the other.

"Now you're too slow," Toots said. "You'll get left behind."

A fat white snowflake fell, plop, on Pip's head. It made him jump. "It tickles!" He giggled.

"Now you're dancing," sighed Toots. "Try not to be so bouncy, Pip."

Pip tumbled on to his belly and slid across the snow. "I'm going to practise on my own," he grumbled. "I can't do it when you're looking at me."

"But everyone will be watching on Christmas morning," his sister said. "Just copy me."

"No," said Pip, and when Toots wasn't watching, he marched off in the other direction, skipping and hopping. And every time a snowflake landed on his head it made him wiggle and giggle.

By midday he'd marched all the way to an enormous wooden house, standing on its own in the middle of the snow. It was painted red and green, and Toots had once told him it was where Santa Claus lived. His elves made presents for all the children, and on Christmas Eve Santa delivered them on his magical, flying sleigh. Santa was outside feeding one of his reindeer.

"Hello," Pip said. "I'm Pip and I'm practising my marching for the Penguin Parade."

"How jolly," said Santa. But he didn't look jolly.

"Is something wrong?" asked Pip.

"One of my elves isn't feeling very well. He's caught a horrible cold."

"Oh dear," said Pip. "Perhaps I can cheer him up! This always makes my sister laugh…" He began to march.

But Santa still looked sad. "I'm sure my elf would love that," he said. "But he's fast asleep. And now I don't have anyone to stuff the teddies for the girls and boys." He shook his head glumly. "I'm worried I won't have my presents ready to deliver on Christmas Eve."

"Oh dear," said Pip. "Shall I stay and help you?" Then he tripped on his feet and fell, splat, in the snow.

"I think you'd better practise your marching, little Pip," said Santa kindly.

Pip waddled off and practised until the sky grew dark, but still he could not get it right.

"Can you march now?" asked Toots, when Pip finally arrived home.

"Of course," fibbed Pip. "I marched all the way to Santa's house. He's a bit sad as one of his elves is not very well and can't stuff the teddies."

"Poor Santa," yawned Toots, falling asleep.

Mum nestled Pip under her flipper. "Time for you to go to bed too, little Pip."

But Pip couldn't sleep. He kept worrying about his marching and Santa Claus, and the girls and boys who might not get their presents. He peeped out from Mum's flipper and looked up at the inky sky. It was glittering with stars. Shiny, silvery, sparkly stars.

I wonder if that's my surprise, thought Pip. *A bucketful of stars!* And he watched them twinkling until he fell asleep, and dreamed of Santa flying his sleigh through a starry sky.

"Wake up, Pip!" Toots squealed, early next morning. "It's Christmas Eve! Only one day till the Penguin Parade. We need to practise our marching."

"Sorry, Toots," said Pip, "but I think I'm going to help Santa instead."

Mum smiled. "Santa will be delighted," she said. "Perhaps you should help too, Toots?"

Toots shook her feathery head. "I need

to keep marching," she said. "I want to be the best in the Penguin Parade."

Pip marched off to help Santa, and every time a snowflake fell on his head he giggled and hopped.

"Look at Pip!" Toots's friends laughed. "He's going to look so silly tomorrow!"

Toots didn't like them saying that. "At least he's practising," she said with a sigh.

Pip pretended not to hear them and marched on to Santa's house.

He knocked on the door. "Hello, Santa," said Pip. "I've come to help you stuff the teddies. I can use my beak like this." He picked up a mouthful of snow.

"How kind," said Santa. "My elves will be pleased."

"Is the poorly elf feeling any better?" asked Pip.

Santa shook his head. "He's still tucked up in bed," he said. "And now some of the other elves are sneezing, too."

Pip followed Santa into his workshop. It was filled with elves in stripy green jackets and red hats, and lots of them were sniffing and sneezing as they hammered and sewed, and wrapped and glued.

"This is Pip," said Santa. "He's come to help."

The elves were surprised to see a penguin. "Hello, Pip," they said, as one of them handed him a red hat. "You'd better have this to keep your head warm. We don't want you catching a cold as well."

"Now I need to go and get the sleigh ready. I'll leave you to it, Pip!" said Santa.

Pip had never worn a hat before. It was a bit big and slipped over one of his eyes. But he felt very grand and soon he was busy stuffing toys. In fact, he worked so hard that he did not notice when day eventually turned into night.

Finally they were finished. They went outside to find Santa.

"We did it!" cried the elves, as they danced round the sleigh, which was piled high with toys. "Thank you, little Pip."

"We wouldn't have managed without you," said Santa. He looked up at the night sky. "The children will be in bed by now. I need to start delivering their presents."

Pip pointed his flipper up at the twinkling stars. "Those are my presents," he said.

"Ho, ho, ho!" Santa Claus laughed. His fat belly jiggled and his rosy cheeks shone. "I don't think so, little Pip."

Pip was pleased to see Santa jolly, but sad that the stars weren't his shiny surprise.

"Cheer up," said Santa, dipping into his sack of presents. "I think you deserve something special to say thank you for helping us." And he handed Pip a gift.

"For me?" asked Pip. It was all wrapped up in paper and ribbon. Pip tore off the wrapping with his beak, and inside was a red tin drum and two wooden drumsticks.

"You can keep the hat as well," said the elves. "Now, you'd better go or you're going to be tired for the Penguin Parade."

"Thank you!" said Pip. "Thank you!"

He set off, banging the drum, and each time he banged he moved his feet and very soon he was marching! And wearing his hat he didn't feel the snowflakes falling, plop, on his head, so he did not giggle and jump.

Just as he reached home, Pip heard a voice far above him. He looked up to see Santa flying through the night sky on his sleigh.

"Good luck tomorrow, little Pip!" Santa called. "You seem to be marching wonderfully."

The following morning, all the penguins lined up for the Penguin Parade. The young penguins were at the front, but they were so excited that they were tripping over their big, webbed feet and marching too fast or too slowly.

"Oh dear," they said, bumping into each other. "What shall we do? All the children are coming to watch us."

Just then, Pip arrived, marching in time to his red tin drum.

"Look at Pip!" said the little penguins. "He's such a good marcher."

"Pip is?" said Toots. "Are you sure?"

"So he is!" said her friends in surprise.

"Perhaps he should lead us?" said the little penguins.

"Absolutely," said Toots. "Will you, Pip? Will you lead the Penguin Parade?"

Pip pulled his red hat on tight and marched up to the front of the group. "Follow me!" he said, banging his drum.

Soon all the penguins were marching behind him. Bouncing and skipping. And hopping and jumping. Especially when the snow began to fall.

"Hooray!" cheered the children. "This is the best Penguin Parade ever!"

"Did you hear that?" whispered Toots.

Pip beamed. "All thanks to Santa," he said. "Because we can march to the tin drum."

Toots shook her head. "All thanks to you, little Pip. Santa wouldn't have given it

24

to you if you hadn't helped him stuff the teddies. And look! All the children have their teddies!"

Pip smiled proudly.

The happy children clapped and cheered as the penguins kept bouncing and marching. "The little penguins are so cute!" they said. "Let's give them their presents!" And they raced forward with brimming buckets.

"Fishes!" Pip giggled.

"Shiny, silvery fishes!" Toots laughed. "Sparkling in the sun. It's your shiny, silvery, sparkly surprise."

"Yippee!" said Pip. "Fishes are so much tastier than stars!"

"Ho, ho, ho!" came a jolly laugh.

Pip saw Santa at the back of the crowd and waved his flipper at him excitedly. "I love surprises!" he cried. "Happy Christmas, Santa! Happy Christmas, Toots! Happy Christmas, everyone!"

Toots chuckled. "Happy Christmas, little Pip!"

FINDING
BIGFOOT

Guy Bass

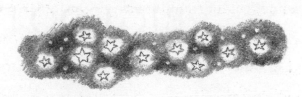

Bigfoot scratched the back of his hairy head and peered into the snow-covered forest. It seemed to stretch in every direction, as far as the eye could see.

"Does I know you, tree?" mumbled the massive, ape-like creature, peering at the trunk of a towering redwood. "Leaves … branches … bark … it *sort of* rings a bell… Has I passed you earlier? Has I been here before?"

The morning sun was still below the treeline, casting shimmering spotlights on the blanket of pristine snow. High above him, a lone woodpecker tap-tap-tapped its rapid rhythm into the tree trunk.

"Remember the teachings of the Old Bigfoots – them of Times Past," Bigfoot said to himself. "The sun rises in the west … no, wait, east. Definitely east! So … which way is east? Oh, all these trees look the same! Boo and begone, you rotten forest!"

Bigfoot slumped down on to a fallen log and put his head in his hands.

"You look lost," chirped a voice. Bigfoot looked up and saw a small red and black woodpecker flutter down on to the log next to him.

"I *is* lost!" sighed Bigfoot. "I doesn't know where I is, where I has been or where I is going. I can't even find my way home."

"Is there anything I can do to help? I don't mean to brag, but we woodpeckers are well known for our sage advice."

"*Strange advice?*" echoed Bigfoot.

"*Sage* – it means wise," said the woodpecker. "Now then – where, if you don't mind me asking, would you like to go?"

"Anywhere!" replied Bigfoot. "I is a Bigfoot, after all. It's what I is supposed to do – wander the Great Forest, leaving mysterious footprints in the snow or giving passers-by a glance of a shaggy shoulder or a hairy hand, before I disappear into the trees... That's what a Bigfoot does – it keeps the Bigfoot myth alive! That's what we has always done, since there's been forests for us to wander."

"Sounds like quite a responsibility," said the woodpecker, fluffing its feathers.

"But ever since the Old Bigfoots of Times Past has moved on, I has this forest all to myself – I has to find my own way," sighed Bigfoot. "Turns out all I is good at doing is getting lost! This whole forest looks the same to me. Left, right, north, south, clockwise, upside-down – it's all just *forest*! How do I know where I has wandered?"

"Does it matter?" asked the woodpecker.

"Of course it does!" grumbled Bigfoot. "If I doesn't know where I has been, how will I know where I is going? Or where I is, for that matter?"

"I suppose you won't. You'll be lost," replied the woodpecker.

"That's what I've been telling you!" growled Bigfoot. "I see how you woodpeckers is known for strange advice – all you do is repeat what I say. I need help! I need to know where I is, where I is going and where I— OW!"

Bigfoot leaped off the log, rubbing his hairy rump.

"What happened?" asked the woodpecker.

"I has been bitten on the bottom!" he yelped, looking down. On the snow-dusted log was a seemingly endless line of army ants, making its way towards him. Leading the march, the largest of the ants gnashed its machete jaws.

"You there!" bellowed Bigfoot. "What's with the bottom-biting?"

"Somebody needed to snap you out of your mopin' mood, you self-pityin' excuse for a mythical creature!" squeaked the army ant. "I can hear your whinin' from a mile away. It's bad for troop morale! Why, this army's been marchin' for days without so much as a toilet break. What's a lazy, gadabout, do-nothing critter like you got to be sad about?"

"I — I is lost," admitted Bigfoot. "I doesn't know where I is, where I has been or where I is going. I can't even find my way home. I is *lost.*"

"Lost? Lost?" cried the army ant. "There ain't no such thing as lost! Why, we army ants are as blind as can be — can't even see the pincers in front of our faces – but do you see us complainin' about being lost? No, sir! You got to learn to follow a *trail*, trooper!"

"Trail?" asked Bigfoot, scratching his beard.

"Of course! We ants leave a trail of stinks and stenches wherever we go," said the army ant. "Now I ain't sayin' you should start tinklin' on the trees, but you're a *Bigfoot* – you leave a trail of footprints wherever you go!"

"Footprints?" repeated Bigfoot. He looked about. Sure enough, the snow was covered in his great, impressive footprints, like a map showing him where he'd been. "But that's ... brilliant! Why hasn't I ever thought of that? I can follow my footprints! I hasn't seen the wood for the trees!"

"Well, I think I've been wagglin' my mandibles long enough," said the army ant, with a quick salute. "Company, by the left – quick march!"

After gratefully waving off the ants, Bigfoot turned back to the woodpecker.

"See? Now that is *proper* advice," he said. "Footprints!"

"True, true," nodded the woodpecker. "But what about when it snows?"

"Hasn't you been listening? The snow is the key! I can follow my footprints! Boo and begone, you stupid bird!"

With that, Bigfoot trudged off into the forest.

The woodpecker shrugged and returned to his tap-tap-tapping.

Bigfoot spent the rest of the day doing his best to wander. Every few steps, he turned around to check that his footprints were nice and clear. Now and again, he would come across a footprint pointing in the opposite direction, and realize he'd accidentally doubled back.

"It works! I know where I is, where I has been and where I is going! I never has to be lost again! Thanks, ants!"

It was nightfall when a delighted Bigfoot finally decided he had done enough wandering for one day. As he still hadn't managed to find his way home, he curled up at the base of a tree, before falling asleep with a smile on his face.

When Bigfoot awoke, he was surprised not to feel the warming light of the morning sun. Instead, he felt rather cold, even under all his thick fur. It took him a moment to realize he was completely covered ... in snow.

Bigfoot sat up, shaking the thick layer of snow off his back. He looked up to see a million snowflakes cascading from the sky —

and then he looked down. The forest was covered in a pristine blanket of bright, new snowfall.

"Oh, *no*," he muttered, rubbing his eyes. "Oh, SNOW! My precious footprints is all covered up!"

He began digging his huge hands into the snow, searching fruitlessly for his buried footprints.

"Oh, what's the use?" he bellowed. "It snows every night in this forest! Any tracks I leave will only get covered. I will be lost again! Boo and begone, you wicked weather!"

Bigfoot fell back into the snow in despair, letting the new snowflakes settle on his fur. After a moment, he heard a familiar tap-tap-tapping. He peered up into the tree, and saw the red and black woodpecker, dutifully pecking away at the tree trunk.

"Woodpecker, you was right!" he cried. "The snow snowed over my footprints and now I is back where I started!"

The woodpecker stopped pecking and fluttered down next to Bigfoot.

"That *is* the problem with snow. I'd offer you some sage advice, but I'm not sure you'd want to hear it," it said, dryly. "Instead I shall let you into a secret I haven't told anyone – if you like."

"Suit yourself," grunted Bigfoot.

The woodpecker ruffled its feathers and picked at a flea under its wing. "Very well, here is my secret. Sometimes I wake up in the morning and I think, oh no, not *more* pecking," revealed the woodpecker. "Peck, peck, peck, all day, every day … to find food, to build my nest, even to call to other woodpeckers – all I do is *peck*! Hammering my poor beak into one tree trunk after another. It isn't easy, you know. I get the most awful headaches…"

"I had no idea," admitted Bigfoot, scratching his beard.

"Why would you? I see all the other birds of the forest, plucking their food off the ground or building their nests out of twigs and leaves they find lying about, or chattering to each other with a tuneful tweet and I think, what a life! Why don't I just do that?

It looks a hundred times easier than bashing my brains out every day."

"Then why—" began Bigfoot.

"Because *that* is what makes me a woodpecker. Not a blackbird or a buzzard or a yellow-browed bunting, not a beaver or a brown bear or even a Bigfoot ... but a *woodpecker*. That's what makes me who I am. And when you put us all together – the animals, birds, insects, trees, plants ... well, that is what makes the forest."

"I suppose," said Bigfoot, running his hand across a snow-dusted leaf.

"And you? You are a Bigfoot. You are the myth ... the mystery of the forest. You are the *wanderer*."

"But what good is wandering if I doesn't

know where I has been, or where I is going, or where I is?" asked Bigfoot. "I can't even find my way home…"

"But you *are* home," replied the woodpecker. "This whole forest is your home – every last tree and stone and patch of grass. Your home stretches in every direction, as far as the eye can see."

"As far as the eye can see…" repeated Bigfoot, thoughtfully.

"Well, I had better get back to work – this tree trunk won't peck itself," said the woodpecker. "Happy wandering, Bigfoot."

Bigfoot watched as the woodpecker flew back up into the high branches of the tree and began tap-tap-tapping like there was no tomorrow. After a moment, he peered again into the endless forest. All of a sudden it looked … different.

He took a deep, cold breath and made his way through the trees. He didn't bother to try to follow his tracks. He just followed his nose wherever it took him.

Within minutes, Bigfoot had no idea where he was, where he'd been or where he was going. He was totally, utterly lost … and he couldn't have been happier.

SEELEY'S SONG

Michael Broad

On the morning of the North Pole Talent Show, animals were arriving from far and wide to perform in their different entertainment categories. Seeley the seal pup watched from the wings as they rehearsed on the stage that had been specially built for that evening's show. He saw a troop of dancing Arctic hares, a band of juggling walruses, and a very large polar bear doing impressions and telling jokes.

Everyone was hoping to impress the seven reindeer judges, and honorary guest Santa Claus – who would invite one lucky act to tour the North Pole in his Christmas Variety Show!

Seeley thought all of the performers were very talented, but he was there to see one act in particular. The Blubber Brothers were singing in the show, and he was hoping to audition for them before their rehearsal and earn a place in the group.

When the three seals bounded into the backstage area, Seeley hurried over to them and approached the lead singer, Bobo. The Blubber Brothers were all older and much bigger than the young seal, and Bobo was by far the biggest.

"My name is Seeley," Seeley panted, peering up at the huge seal. "I love to sing more than anything else in the world and I would like to audition to join the Blubber Brothers!"

"You're just a fluffy little pup," scoffed Bobo, roughly ruffling Seeley's downy white fur and making the other seals snigger. "We're not called the Blubber Babies, you know!"

"I know," pleaded Seeley. "But if you give me a chance—"

"What do you sing, anyway?" interrupted Bobo.

"Nursery rhymes!" jeered the others.

"Let me show you," said Seeley, and cleared his throat.

The little pup began singing his favourite song in his own unique, high-pitched voice. It was a song he'd made up himself about how he loved to sing and longed to share his music with the world. But Seeley only managed to utter the first few lines before Bobo flopped on to his back and began roaring with laughter. Soon all of the Blubber Brothers were rolling around the ice, flapping their flippers and howling, completely drowning out Seeley's song.

"You sound like a little girl!" sneered Bobo, making fun of the young pup's high voice. "Maybe you should find a group called the Blubber Sisters, because we *definitely* don't want you!"

This sent the Blubber Brothers into another fit of laughter before they bounded away for their rehearsal, leaving the fluffy little seal with his feelings hurt and his dreams crushed.

Seeley felt tears welling up in his eyes, so he hurried across the ice and dived into the water where no one would see him. The Blubber Brothers had teased him, but the little seal still believed in his music and continued the song beneath the waves.

"I wish that I could sing a song
For everyone to hear,
A song to make them joyful
Whenever clouds appear,
A song that they can turn to
Whenever things go wrong,
And I will make them happy
With my merry little song."

Seeley sang in his unusually high voice. And as he sang, he heard the sound of someone humming in harmony. The other voice was low and deep.

"Hmmm, hmm, mmm," it sang. *"Hmmm, mm, mm, mm..."*

Seeley thought the humming was wonderful. It had to come from someone who shared his love of music! He continued to sing as he swam through a maze of underwater ice-tunnels, following the melody as it echoed through the ocean.

Eventually the tunnel led into open water where the little seal found a gigantic blue whale! She was swimming in circles and twirling around, humming to herself as she danced to his song. Seeley was so amazed by her size that he stopped singing suddenly, which surprised the whale and so she stopped too.

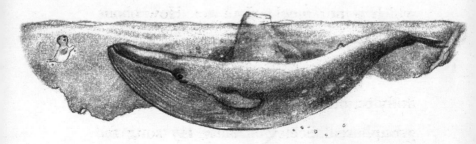

"I didn't mean to disturb you," gasped the seal. "My name's Seeley."

"I'm Bella," said the whale. "Was that your song I was humming along to?"

"Yes," he replied shyly. "Are you rehearsing for the North Pole Talent Show?"

"Oh, I wish I was!" replied Bella.

"You should take part," said Seeley. "Why don't you?"

"Because the stage is on land and much too small for someone my size," explained Bella. "And I can only really hum and dance, which is not much of an act. How about you, are you in the show?"

"I wanted to be, but I was too small and fluffy to join the Blubber Brothers' singing group," said Seeley. "I sang my song for them, but they said my voice was too high."

"I think your voice is lovely!" said Bella.
"And so is your song."

"I really like your humming and
dancing," said Seeley.

Bella and Seeley were quiet for a
moment, and then they both spoke at the
same time.

"We should form an act together!" they
said.

Even if they couldn't enter the talent
show, the seal and the whale decided they
could still perform for their own enjoyment.
They sang and made up dance routines –
and together they had the most fun ever!

As the evening drew in and the sky grew
dark, Bella and Seeley swam to the surface

and watched as the distant stage lights were switched on and the audience began taking their places for the show.

"I wish we could have entered the talent show as a singing and dancing duet," said Bella, peeping above the waterline. "Your song is so wonderful, I'm sure the audience would have loved it."

"Can you imagine performing for Santa Claus?" added Seeley.

"The stage wouldn't last very long with me twirling on it!" Bella laughed. "Though there's probably still time for you to enter on your own as a solo singer."

"I wouldn't want to sing without you," said Seeley, who'd had the most amazing day sharing music with his brand-new friend.

"I just wish there was some way we could enter together."

Seeley and Bella watched as the audience finally settled and the reindeer judges took their places at the side of the stage. Then Santa Claus stepped up to the microphone, welcomed the audience and wished everyone the best of luck.

"And I will invite the act with the most seasonal spirit to join us on the road in our Christmas Variety Show," he said, to massive applause from the audience. "Now let the North Pole Talent Show begin!"

Out to sea, where no one could see them, Seeley and Bella had a brilliant view of the stage. They sang along with the songs and danced to the music, they laughed at the comedy, and clapped and cheered for all the winners and losers.

The juggling walruses won first place in the variety category, and the very large polar bear scooped the best comedy performance. The Blubber Brothers lost out to a pack of howling wolves for best singing group and were last seen trailing behind Bobo as he stormed off the stage.

Towards the end of the show, the reindeer judges huddled together with Santa to discuss which act had the most seasonal spirit and who would be invited to tour the North Pole in Santa's Christmas Variety Show.

Seeley and Bella were wondering which lucky act would be chosen, when they noticed the audience members shifting about and turning their heads towards the sea. Some seemed to be pointing in their direction, while others simply stared, wide-eyed with amazement.

"Are they looking at us?" whispered Seeley, feeling self-conscious.

"I don't think so... Look!" said Bella, seeing bright pink and green colours flickering across the sky, swirling and dancing above her friend. "The Northern Lights are putting on a show of their own tonight!"

"WOW!" gasped Seeley.

Soon everyone in the audience had shuffled around and was gazing out to sea, even Santa and the reindeer judges, who broke from their huddle to watch the spectacle.

"Do you think they can see us?" asked Seeley.

"I don't think so," said Bella. "But the Nothern Lights aren't at their brightest yet. Soon they'll illuminate the sky and the sea, too. Then no one will be able to miss us!"

"Brilliant!" said Seeley, and he smiled at his friend.

Bella frowned, but then her eyes lit up.

With everyone looking out to sea, Seeley and Bella had a chance to perform together in the North Pole Talent Show. All they needed was a spectacular entrance to get everyone's attention.

Bella dived down to the seabed with Seeley holding on to her fin, and as the colourful sky grew even brighter, she swam towards the surface. Seeley held on tight as they soared through the air, their water trail illuminated by the Northern Lights.

The audience gasped as they plunged back into the sea, and then held their breath, hoping the pair would return.

Moments later, the seal pup rose majestically from the water on the head of the giant blue whale, who was flapping her fins gracefully and swimming in circles.

With the Northern Lights swirling in the starry sky, the duo performed Seeley's song, their unusual voices in perfect harmony.

"I wish that I could sing a song
For everyone to hear,
A song to make them joyful
Whenever clouds appear..."

The colours in the sky seemed to move
in time to the music, and when the song
finished the audience erupted with cheers
and applause.

Santa and the reindeers huddled together once again and quickly decided that the seal and the whale should be invited to tour the North Pole with the Christmas Variety Show.

"Bringing joy to others is the true spirit of Christmas," Santa told Seeley and Bella, to the delight of the audience and the other acts. "And I would be honoured if you would join our show."

"Our wish came true!" said Bella, twirling in the sea.

"Now we really will get to sing for everyone to hear!" said Seeley.

The seal pup and the whale became a singing sensation, touring the North Pole with Santa's Christmas Variety Show, but it didn't end there. Word spread fast about the unusual duo and they went on to tour the world, and animals came from far and wide to see Bella dance and to hear Seeley's song.

DOG STAR

Caroline Pitcher

Blue-eyed Chookie the husky pup wagged her fluffy tail as the man led her out of the shed. Today she would pull the sledge with her pack for the very first time. The other dogs pawed with excitement at the snow, but Chookie whined nervously.

"Don't worry, pup," said a black and white dog called Nanook. "There's a first time for all of us. And our man and his children are kind."

"But I'm frightened of *him*," whispered Chookie. "I'm frightened of Luther."

Luther lived indoors with the man and his family. Now he stared at Chookie with his odd, slanting eyes, one amber and one ice-blue. He padded over to her.

"We are the best sledge pack there is, pup," Luther growled softly. "Make sure you are the best, too. Run fast and well and be faithful to your pack. Always."

Chookie lowered her head obediently. *Yes, I will.*

Chookie heard the man's big boots creaking on the snow as he harnessed his dog team. He was dressed in bearskin trousers and a thick padded anorak. His girl and boy ran up, wearing clothes of warm sealskin for the journey. Their wind-burned faces were circled by the thick white fur trimming their hoods.

"Come on, Chookie," said the man. "Let's put you with the experts." He harnessed her in a row of three beside Nanook and a brown and white dog called Kree. Luther the Pack Leader was right at the front.

"It's your first real run, Chookie!" cried the girl, and Chookie wagged her tail in happiness.

"We're going fishing!" cried the boy.

The other huskies bayed and leaped in a frenzy, desperate to run together across the snow lands.

"Hey-*yoh*! *Mush!*" called the man, and they were off at last.

Chookie felt the rush of wind past her ears. She heard the crunch of the sledge's runners on the snow. Could she keep up? *Yes, she could!* The team ran so fast, yet her snow-paws gripped the ground without slipping. Below her was the crystal white snow. Above her the sky was the deep, deep blue of mountain flowers. This was pure joy. This was what she was born for, to be one of a pack, all running at the same speed with the sledge skimming over the snow behind them.

"Hey-*yoh!*" called the man. His whip cracked high above the huskies' backs, but it never touched them. When he steered them right or left, twelve strong tails swung together. The perfect team.

The huskies raced along the edge of a forest of tall, straight trees. Ahead was the bay where the frozen sea met the land. The ice shone silver-blue in the winter light.

"*Whoa!*" called the man, and the huskies slowed down until at last they stopped. They stood with pink tongues lolling from their jaws and their breath clouding in the icy air.

The man climbed off the sledge. He strode to the frozen bay and crouched down. "The ice is too thin now," he said. "It won't hold our sledge as it did in the old days."

He unclipped the huskies.

"Stay here!" Luther the Leader commanded them. Chookie sat, content, knowing that so far she had run well.

The man took his backpack and strode towards the silver bay. His children tumbled down on to the snow and ran after him. Chookie watched, ears pricked, as the man took a shovel. He hacked and cut until he had made a circular hole in the ice. The children squatted on the ice, and held their breath as he lowered in a line with a hook. The line quivered and the children cheered as their father pulled it up with a fish on the end. Again and again, the man dropped the line. Again and again, he caught a fish, and his children cheered.

Chookie lay down on the snow, her head on her paws. The time passed slowly when she was not running.

The man stood up. The children ran back to where the huskies waited and took dry wood from a sack. They built it into a pyramid, then the man strode back and lit it. Chookie smelled the wood catch fire and saw the smoke puff into the cold air. She liked the feel of the fire's warmth on her body. The man began to cook the fish, and Chookie heard it crackle and blister on the flames. Her mouth watered and drooled in hunger at the smell.

"It's no use slobbering, pup," said Nanook. "We have to wait until the humans have finished. Rest now, ready for the run back."

Chookie watched the man serve fish to his children on blue enamel plates. They ate their hot food with a lot of lip-smacking. The man told them a story about a polar bear and her cubs, and afterwards the children dozed. Then he unfastened the huskies' harnesses and the older dogs lay down, even Luther. They closed their eyes and slept.

Chookie sniffed the cold air. She could still smell the fish. *Mmm...* She shuffled down into the snow. The cold would take a while to get past her strong, thick fur and the soft down below it. Chookie put her nose down and closed her eyes, but it was no good. She couldn't settle.

What was that? There was a white flurry over towards the forest. Something was kicking up the snow. Something was moving. It was not big enough to be a reindeer and it was too far from the bay to be a seal. Perhaps it was a fox? Chookie had to chase after whatever it was, she just could not help herself! She was off and away, dashing pell-mell across the snow.

The creature knew she was coming and kicked up a little blizzard in the snow as it turned and ran. Chookie saw a flurry of long feet and the tips of two ears. *A hare! An Arctic hare!* It bounded along the edge of the forest, keeping to the line of trees. At the last moment, it turned sharp right and disappeared into the forest. Chookie raced after it. It was darker here, because the daylight could not reach through the thick roof of branches. Chookie had to slow down, and weave in and out between the trees, keeping her blue eyes fixed on the hare. If she looked away for even an instant, she would lose it.

But as she headed further into the forest, Chookie knew something was not right. She should not be here by herself. She should be with the other huskies. What had he said, Luther, the stern Pack Leader with his odd slanting eyes? *Be faithful to your pack. Always.*

The ground shook. Chookie glanced over her shoulder. There stood a huge moose, swaying his great antlers. He glared at Chookie, put his head down, blew through his nostrils and stamped his huge snowshoe hoof again. Chookie wished Nanook was here, so she could ask her if a moose was dangerous. She slowed and ran half a circle, well out of the reach of those big antlers.

But, oh! Where was the hare now? *Nowhere to be seen.* It had vanished into the depths of the forest.

Chookie turned and loped back through the trees. She had been so intent on chasing that hare she had not realized how far she had run.

Ah! The trees were thinning. Chookie ran out of the forest, expecting it to be lighter, but while she had been chasing that hare, the short day had ended. Outside it was almost as dark as in the forest.

Where was the icy bay? Where was the sledge with the kind man and his children? Where was her pack?

Chookie sniffed the air hopefully, but she could not find their scent. She stood gazing across the snowy wastes, one forepaw raised, ready to run, if only she knew which way to go.

A cold splodge landed on her nose. Slowly, snowflakes began to circle, as if they were waltzing down from the sky. More and more snowflakes joined the dance until they filled the air and Chookie could see nothing but snow. The snowflakes were white, but there were so many thousands of them that they looked as dark as soot. A cold wind began to whip them into a faster dance. It blew furrows in the snow already on the ground, and furrows in Chookie's fur, too.

She was so hungry. The rest of her pack would have eaten their fish by now. They would creep nearer to the fire to warm their sides and their full tummies. Oh! Chookie wanted to be back with them so much. She put back her head and howled, but the unkind wind took her howl and whisked it far away. Her cry was lost in the snowstorm and her pack would never hear her.

Chookie shivered. She needed shelter.

She curled up into a tight ball and wrapped her tail over her paws. She dozed.

When she opened her eyes again, the snowflakes' dance was over. The air was still. She looked up. The sky was clear and black, and as she stared, bright stars appeared, fizzing out from the darkness.

Together the stars flickered and made a shape against the sky. It was a shape she knew well. She had seen it before. It was the shape of a dog, made of stars.

How I wish you could lead me to my pack, Dog Star!

Chookie got to her feet, put back her head and called to the dog in the sky, with a howl full of longing. She waited, and then called again, such a sad and mournful howl.

And there was an answer! Not just one dog howling in reply, but many, one after the other, on different notes. It was a choir of dogs, singing to *her*.

Chookie sang back, and waited. The dog choir sang again. It was not singing up in the sky among the stars.

It was somewhere nearby.

Chookie followed the sound. Never had she run so fast. She saw the ice on the bay gleam silver in the starlight. The Dog Star was showing her the way.

A little further on, Chookie skidded to a stop. She threw back her head and howled, and the dog choir answered almost at once. They sounded much, much nearer. Chookie dashed towards that wonderful sound. And there they were, her pack. The man fetched the fish he had saved just for her and the boy and girl ran to pat her.

"Chookie!" cried the girl. "Thank goodness! We searched for you, but we had to come back here to shelter from the storm."

"It was clever of you to howl and tell us where you were," cried the boy.

"Well done, pup!" yelped Nanook. The huskies wagged their strong tails to welcome their youngest one.

But what about Luther, the Pack Leader?

Chookie trembled. She lowered her head and then glanced up at his stern face with its odd eyes, one amber, one blue.

"Welcome back, Chookie," he said. "You've learned a lot today. You have come back to us. You have been faithful to your pack."

Chookie wagged her tail at last, so thankful to be home amongst them. She looked up at the dark sky.

Thank you, Dog Star.

THE WISH
ELEPHANT

Elizabeth Baguley

Louisa took the oddly-shaped package from Papa carefully, with both hands.

"I thought that you should have at least one Christmas decoration, even though we're abroad," said Papa, as Louisa unwrapped the final layer of tissue paper.

Nestled within was a heavy glass ball on a china stand. It was filled with clear liquid, and inside was a perfect copy of Full Moon House, the home which Louisa and Mama and Papa had left behind in England. It had the same arched windows, the same round turret, the same high roof with its pointed gables – all so different from this horrible, low, flat-roofed *bungalow*, which lay amongst a jigsaw of endless tea fields. A homesick lump swelled in Louisa's throat.

"Shake it," said Papa.

Louisa tipped the glass ball upside down. Inside, a flurry of tiny white flecks was stirred up into a storm before settling gently on the roof of Full Moon House. "It's a snow-globe." Papa smiled.

"Oh, thank you," said Louisa. "It's just like h…" She could say no more.

Papa gave her his handkerchief, then patted her shoulder rather awkwardly, before hurrying off to talk to his workers. Now Louisa was alone, she let her tears fall quietly. She loved the snow-globe, of course – Papa and Mama must have brought it all the way to India on the ship. But it made her long to be looking out at the view of Christmas snow from her own pretty room in England.

"I wish…" she whispered, but stopped herself. What was the use of wishing? Papa needed to be in India because of his job and there was no going back.

Louisa shook the globe again and watched the flakes fall. Last year, Full Moon House had looked just like this, its roof padded with snow. On Christmas Day cheery fires had been lit in every room.

Holly and ivy were wound around the bannisters, and they had decorated a fir tree with a galaxy of tiny candles. After church, they had eaten a fine meal of roast goose and plum pudding, then, as a special treat, Louisa had been allowed to stay up, and Papa and Mama had taken her skating on the frozen river, wearing her very own skates. Oh, the icy thrill of it!

There would be no skating this Christmas. Papa said that in India snow only fell in the high mountains in the north, far, far away from here. From the covered walkway around the house, which she had learned to call the *verandah*, Louisa could see a haze of heat quivering above the tea bushes in the fields beyond the garden. Lakshmi, her *ayah* (so different from stiff old Miss Forrest, her governess in England) always smiled at Louisa's complaints about the heat. If Louisa was hot now, she should wait to see what it was like in the summer!

Christmas in this country didn't feel like Christmas at all.

Lakshmi came towards her saying,

"Miss, we are going to the market now." She slid the precious snow-globe into her little velvet bag, and followed her nursemaid down into the garden.

The market was an explosion of nose-tickling smells and mingled sounds. Chickens clucked in pens, a chattering monkey clung to its owner's back. A rainbow of strange vegetables and odd fruits lay in piles on the ground, amongst them bunches of *kayla*, yellow and curved. The skin was thick and had to be peeled off in strips, but inside the cream-coloured flesh was sweet and soft. As usual, Lakshmi bought some and gave one to Louisa to eat later.

A crowd had gathered at the edge of the marketplace. In the small space amid the jostling people was an elephant. He made Louisa feel small, even though Lakshmi said that he was only young. His trunk swung this way and that, but he stood quietly while the crowd stared and babbled around him.

"This elephant is special: he is *kasi.* It means bright or white," said Lakshmi.

Louisa thought that the animal looked faded, like the ghost of an elephant.

"He can give wishes," said Lakshmi.

Louisa thought that the elephant might want to make a wish himself – a wish to escape from the chain which fastened him to a tree. The crowd jostled and prodded him and the *mahout* – his keeper – had a stick.

A loud cry pierced the market hubbub and a man skidded through the market, chased by many others, shouting and running.

"A thief!" shouted Lakshmi. "Miss, we will follow to see this excitement."

"I can't run – I have to be careful of my snow—" said Louisa. But Lakshmi and the rest of the crowd had gone, leaving Louisa and the elephant alone.

How patient but sad he looked, the finger-like tip of his trunk pulling at the chain around his leg.

"Here," said Louisa, moving closer. "Have this." She held out the *kayla* towards the elephant. Gently, the elephant gripped the fruit and ate it. Louisa laughed as the trunk reached towards her for more.

"All gone!" She smiled. The elephant, though, had other ideas. His trunk searched around before opening the flap of her velvet bag and pulling out the snow-globe.

"Oh no!" gasped Louisa. "That's not for you!" She caught her breath as the elephant held the globe close to its short-sighted eyes.

"Please," she begged, holding out her hands. "It's the only snow I have." The elephant made a low sound as though he understood, then gave the globe back.

"Thank you, *Kasi!*" she cried, remembering the word Lakshmi had used. "I'll bring you another *kayla* soon."

Lakshmi was suddenly running back towards her, shouting at the *mahout* to keep his beast away from the English Miss. "He will run wild and carry her away," she cried out.

"He's not hurting me!" Louisa shouted, but the *mahout* was pushing through the crowd, waving his stick.

Louisa began to tug uselessly at Kasi's chain. "Oh, I wish you could escape," she said, stroking his side. As she did so, she felt a warm tingling in her hands and when she pulled at the chain again, suddenly – somehow – it was broken. Kasi swung away through the market, now a frenzy of running and diving, gabbling and shrieking as the people fled from the escaped elephant. Kasi stepped delicately through it all, simply heading away into the trees beyond the marketplace. *I hope you'll be safe*, thought Louisa, as he disappeared towards the forest, where he belonged.

"Bad elephant!" exclaimed Lakshmi. But Louisa didn't think he was bad at all – like her, he just wanted to go home.

At supper, back in the stuffy bungalow, Louisa sat quietly staring at the snow-globe as if it might suddenly transport her to the real Full Moon House.

"Let's play charades – as we always do in England on Christmas Eve," Mama suggested. But even though Papa joined in, it still didn't feel like Christmas at all.

When bedtime came, Louisa was too hot to sleep so she slipped barefoot into the garden, taking the snow-globe with her, trying to conjure up the shivery feeling of Christmas Eve. She sat on the lawn and shook the globe, then set it down to watch the flakes glitter in the moonlight. She hummed a carol to herself and imagined the rumbling sound of the church organ back home. Soon she was lost in the dream of a candlelit fir tree and the bright presents under it and Papa's kind hand on her shoulder...

There was a sudden sound as deep as the organ, and Louisa did indeed feel something on her shoulder, but it was not Papa's hand. It was a trunk. There was an elephant in the garden! She leaped up and tried to run, but her feet seemed stuck. She twisted, tripped over her nightgown and landed face down on the grass. Before she could scream, she was being lifted by a strong trunk and placed back on her feet. There before her stood the creature, its skin glowing pale as a ghost.

"Kasi!" she exclaimed. Surely this gentle

beast would never hurt her. Kasi flapped his ears as though he knew his name, then swiftly wrapped his trunk around her and placed her safely on his back. Then he was moving away from the garden, through the tea plantation and into the forest. They were going so fast that it felt almost as though they were skimming on the wind or swimming through moonlight, going so fast that everything whirled into a blur.

At last, Kasi slowed and the world settled into focus. Against the dark sky stood jagged silver peaks. "Mountains!" Louisa breathed. Yet Papa had told her that the mountains were in the north. How could they have travelled so far so soon? Kasi was lifting her to the ground – a ground whiter than starlight and soft as a cloud, so soft that Louisa was sinking into it.

Snow! Real snow – glittery and cold and moon-bright.

Louisa moulded a handful into a perfect ball and threw it high into the air. Kasi dipped his trunk into the feathery whiteness and blew it out in a great sneeze. Then he was rolling in the snow and Louisa was dancing in the snow and it felt like winter. No, not like winter, like…

"…Christmas!" shouted Louisa, as more snow began to fall. It was perfect.

Just when she felt that she was too tired to throw one more snowball, Kasi was settling her on to his back, and the strange, whirling feeling as he sped along muffled her thoughts once more.

At last, Kasi lowered Louisa to the ground outside the bungalow. She stroked Kasi's side and he in turn wrapped his trunk around her, before stepping lightly from the moonlit garden and away towards the plantation.

"Thank you," she whispered after him into the darkness, so glad the little white elephant had shown her that India was a place of magical secrets.

It was Christmas morning. Strangely, in spite of her night-time adventure, Louisa didn't feel tired at all. And somehow the heat didn't feel so bad today, as though snowflakes were fluttering somewhere inside her, keeping her cool.

Snowflakes – oh! The snow-globe! It must still be out on the lawn.

Sure enough, there it was, lying amongst the grass, misted with morning dew. Louisa rubbed it with her handkerchief, then shook it, hardly believing her eyes. The snow-specks fell as before – not on to a tall house with arched windows and a turret, but on to a long, flat-roofed house with a *verandah.*

And standing next to this bungalow was a miniature elephant with skin as pale as a ghost.

Papa came out as she stared in disbelief. "Ah, the snow-globe. Dear old Full Moon House. Still wishing you were home for Christmas?" he asked.

"No, Papa," Louisa replied, hoping that wherever Kasi was now he was as happy as she was. "I *am* home. Merry Christmas."

FERGUS FOX'S CHRISTMAS

Karen Wallace

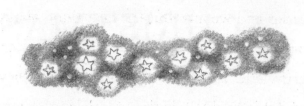

Fergus Fox lived with his mother and his sister, Twitch, at the bottom of the garden of an empty house at Number 33, Hope Road.

It was a brilliant place to live, and the only home that Fergus and Twitch had ever known. There were lots of trees with tunnels under their roots and thick hedges to crawl through. In the summer, the grass grew long because there was no one to cut it, and so it was full of nice things to eat like beetles and worms. But the best thing about Hope Road was the café on the corner. Fergus and Twitch thought it was their very own takeaway! While they waited in the den, Mrs Fox jumped over the hedge and looked through the bins. On a good night, she came home with leftover hamburgers, leftover fish and chips or leftover sausage rolls.

Fergus liked hamburgers, and Twitch chose fish and chips. But they ate anything Mrs Fox brought them.

"A fox can't be a fussy eater," Mrs Fox always said.

The only times when there wasn't much food to be found was when the rubbish men came and Mr Lard, who owned the café, cleaned out the dustbins with bleach. It left a horrible taste which none of the Fox family liked.

One morning in December, Fergus woke up early. The air was colder than he had ever known. He crept up to the entrance of the den. It was still dark, but there was a bright moon in the sky, and to Fergus's amazement the ground was white as if it was covered in chicken feathers.

"Wake up, Mum!" he cried. "Look at the feathers! There must be hundreds of chickens in the garden."

"*Thousands*," said Twitch. Her black eyes glittered. "I can almost *taste* them."

"Those aren't feathers," said Mrs Fox. "That's *snow!*"

"Wow!" cried Fergus. "Does it always snow when it gets cold?"

Mrs Fox laughed. "Not always! But snow makes Christmas seem extra special."

"What's *snow*?" asked Twitch.

"What's *Christmas*?" asked Fergus.

So Mrs Fox told them that snow is what happens when rain gets so cold it turns to ice, and that Christmas is when people put up sparkly decorations in their homes, and a man called Santa Claus, who has a white beard and wears a red suit, brings everyone presents. And there is always a huge Christmas dinner of turkey and sausages and mashed potato with gravy.

Fergus felt his heart banging in his chest and his mouth watering! It seemed to him that Christmas was the best thing ever!

That night Fergus couldn't sleep. He wanted to explore the other houses in the street and see the sparkly decorations and maybe even find something special to eat.

He turned to Twitch and prodded her with his paw. "Wake up!" he whispered. "I want to go on an adventure!"

Twitch opened one sleepy eye. "What kind of adventure?"

"A Christmas adventure," said Fergus. He looked over to where their mother was sleeping soundly. "To look inside the other houses," he added in an excited voice.

Twitch's eyes opened wide. "You mean go outside our garden?"

"Why not?" asked Fergus bravely.

Twitch frowned. "We'll have to ask Mum in the morning."

At first Mrs Fox said no, because it was too dangerous and they might get lost. But Fergus asked again and again, and in the end, Mrs Fox agreed. After all, the two cubs had to go out on their own one day and they were just about old enough.

"All right," she said. "You can go, but don't cross the road, don't talk to strange cats and whatever you do, stay away from dogs."

So Fergus and Twitch promised they would be very careful, and that evening they crept out of the den. They set off across the garden and squeezed under the next-door hedge to see the sparkly decorations for themselves.

It was all very exciting and just a little bit scary!

The first house was all shut up so they decided to go on to the next one. But that was no good either. The lights were on, but the curtains were drawn and it was impossible to see inside.

"Do you think we should go back?"

asked Twitch nervously. "We're two gardens away from home now."

"Third time lucky," said Fergus. "Let's try one more house."

They crawled on their bellies under the hedge and found themselves in the next garden. There were lots of huge plantpots and a stone pond. And the end of the house had big glass doors. It was perfect! Fergus and Twitch could see right inside. They went all the way up to the back of the house and hid behind an extra large plant pot.

Sure enough, Mrs Fox was right! The room was decorated with strings of tiny silver bells and in one corner there was a tree with a star on the top, covered in glass balls all the colours of the rainbow.

A woman was sitting on a chair with a boy and a girl on her lap. She was holding a book with a picture of a man in a red suit driving a sleigh.

"That's Santa Claus," whispered Fergus to Twitch. "Remember, Mum told us about him."

Twitch nodded. The sleigh in the picture was full of parcels wrapped in bright paper. "Do you think those parcels are presents?" she asked.

"Definitely," said Fergus and his eyes shone.

"Santa Claus has lots of reindeer to pull him along," said the children's mother, turning the page.

"I left Santa and his reindeer some food," said the boy, pointing to the fireplace.

In front of the grate was a plate of mince pies, a glass of apple juice and some carrots for the reindeer.

"Do you think Santa will eat two pies or three?" asked the girl.

"I think he'll eat all of them," said the boy. "It's hard work carrying all those presents." He looked at his sister. "Have you made your wish?"

The girl nodded. "Have you?"

"Yes," said the boy firmly. "And it's something I want more than anything else in the whole world."

Their mother smiled and put down the book. "Then I'm sure Santa will bring it, darling. Now off to bed. It will be a busy day tomorrow."

She stood up and led the children out of the room. Then she turned, switched off the light and followed them upstairs.

Twitch and Fergus sat in the dark for a moment. They were both thinking of the presents that Santa was going to bring.

"No one's ever brought me a present," said Fergus to Twitch. "I mean a real present. Not just leftover fish and chips or a bit of hamburger bun."

Twitch looked at him with shiny eyes. "What present would you ask for?"

Fergus thought of something that he really wanted more than anything else in the whole world. "Guess!" he said.

"A feast," said Twitch.

They both laughed because everyone knows that foxes are always hungry.

"Come on," said Fergus. "Mum should be back with supper by now."

But Mrs Fox only had some stale cheese sandwiches because the bin men had empted all the bins outside the café.

"I'm sorry," she said, after everything had been eaten. "It's not much of a supper, but I'll go out and find something nice tomorrow. There'll be lots of leftovers from everyone's Christmas dinners."

But Fergus didn't want other people's leftovers, he had set his heart on a feast of their own and he was determined to have one. "I'll make a Christmas wish," he said. "That's what the children did!"

Twitch yawned. "Maybe Santa Claus doesn't bring presents to foxes."

"Of course he does!" cried Fergus. "All we have to do is ask!"

But Twitch had already curled up in the corner. "You ask," she said. "I'm going to sleep."

Fergus turned to his mother. "What do you think, Mum?"

"Anything's worth a try, Fergus." Mrs Fox yawned. "Don't stay up too late."

Fergus crawled out of the den. The air was completely still and the ground was white as far as he could see. A big silver moon hung in the sky.

It seemed to Fergus that it was the perfect night for making a wish. He looked up and saw a shape moving across the sky, then he heard the faint tinkling of bells.

Something came closer and closer… It was a sleigh pulled by reindeer and Santa Claus was driving! Without a sound, the sleigh landed on the roof of the children's house.

Fergus squeezed his eyes shut and made a wish.

Please! Please, Santa Claus! If foxes get presents, give us a feast for Christmas!

When Fergus opened his eyes, the sleigh was gone, but there was a trail of silver stars sparkling in the air above the den.

The next morning, Fergus was in a deep sleep when Twitch patted him with his paw. "Wake up!" she whispered. "Something wonderful has happened!"

Fergus sat up and his eyes went as round as saucers.

On the other side of the den was a red and green rug edged with silver and gold. And on it was the biggest feast Fergus had ever seen! There was a turkey surrounded by sausages, a roast ham, a bowl of carrots, a bowl of peas, a big dish of fluffy mashed potatoes covered in thick brown gravy and a Christmas pudding.

Fergus's nose twitched like mad! It smelled absolutely fantastic!

The three foxes sat down in a circle on the rug and Mrs Fox passed around three fat sausages.

"I would like to propose a toast," she cried, holding up her sausage in the air.

"To my two clever fox cubs and our happy home on Hope Road."

Twitch held up her sausage. "Here's to Fergus! And his Christmas wish!" she cried.

"Here's to Santa Claus!" shouted Fergus, with a big grin on his face. "And a Happy Christmas to us all!"

Then he threw his sausage in the air and swallowed it in one go!

MORNING
BEAR

Malachy Doyle

"Morning, bear," said Jenny Edwards to the happy little face of the toy in the junk shop window. It was the first time her mum had let her walk to her new school by herself.

"Morning, bear," she called out every morning after, skipping past.

So Morning Bear became the teddy's name. Jenny wanted to own him more than anything in the whole wide world, but she didn't have any money – not even enough for a raggedy old bear.

"Hello again, Morning Bear," she'd say,
on her way home. "I'll see you later, maybe."

And she did, every night in her dreams.

"Morning, Morning Bear!" she called, early
one cold December morning.

Jenny stopped to look more closely at
the shop window. Next to her lovely

bear, there was a
beautiful gingerbread
house. And next to
that was a little
Christmas tree,
all decorated with
bows and candles.

"*Guten Morgen*, young girl," came a voice, from inside. "I'm Mr Hoffman and this is my shop. What did you just call my bear?"

"My lovely Morning Bear!" Jenny answered.

"Why?" asked the old German shopkeeper, coming to the door.

"Because that's his name, like mine's Jenny," she said, before skipping off to school. "And because I love him with all my heart."

From then on the shopkeeper was always there, standing in the doorway, whenever she came past.

"Morning, Mr Hoffman! Morning, Morning Bear!" she called.

"*Guten Morgen*, Jenny," came the reply.

One day, just before Christmas, he called her over. "I know how much you like my bear," he said, "for you always say hello…"

"He's the best bear in all the world," said Jenny. "Oh, Mr Hoffman, I'm so scared someone will buy him one day and he won't be here any more."

"Come inside a minute, Jenny – I think he might like to meet you."

Jenny stepped through the shop door, and Mr Hoffman reached into the window.

"Would you like to hold him?"

"Oh, yes please," Jenny gasped. "I'd love to!"

Morning Bear was old and beautiful and his fur was rubbed thin in all the right places.

"Oh, Mr Hoffman…" She snuggled the little teddy bear close. "I so wish I could take him home with me, but I *know* I'll never have enough money to buy him."

"I'm afraid you couldn't anyway, Jenny, for he's not for sale. He never has been."

"But why is he in the window, then? I thought everything in shop windows was for sale."

"Oh no." Mr Hoffman shook his head. "Not in my shop, anyway. Some things are just there to make people smile as they go past, like the Christmas tree."

"And the gingerbread house?" asked Jenny.

The old man nodded. "My bear lives in the window because he likes to watch the world go by. But no, I could never sell him. He was mine when I was a little boy, in Germany. I still take him home with me every night, so he doesn't get lonely."

"You must like him a lot," said Jenny.

"I do. But I've been thinking maybe, after all these long years, he might want to be with a child again. A child who loves him as much as I do."

Jenny smiled at the bear, and the bear seemed to smile back. "*I* love him, Mr Hoffman," she said quietly.

"I know you do, Jenny. And I'm going to set you a challenge. The same one I've given to the other children who've wanted him over the years…"

Jenny held her breath.

"To be allowed to take him home with you and keep him for ever," the shopkeeper continued, "you'll have to guess his real name. The one I gave him when I was a boy."

"Oh, Morning Bear," Jenny said that night, as she and the bear flew over the rooftops in her dreams. "What did Mr Hoffman call you all those years ago when he was young? I wish you'd tell me."

But Morning Bear only smiled, for how can teddy bears talk?

"*Guten Morgen*, Jenny," said the old man, the next day. "Have you guessed his real name yet?"

Jenny shook her head. There were so many names in the world she didn't know where to start.

"I'll give you a clue," said the shopkeeper. "Of all the children who've tried to guess, you're the warmest already."

Jenny frowned. "What do you mean?" she asked. But Mr Hoffman said no more.

Jenny spent the whole day at school thinking of names – names like Morning Bear. For if she was the warmest already, she thought, it must be something a bit like that.

She pushed open the door of the shop on her way home. "Mr Hoffman, is it Afternoon Bear or Evening Bear or Night Bear? Or maybe it's Dream Bear?"

"It's none of those, I'm afraid." He smiled at her.

"What about Dawn Bear or Sunrise Bear or Breakfast Bear or Cornflake Bear?" she asked him, the next morning.

"Sorry, Jenny," he replied, with a laugh. "It isn't any of those, either."

"But it is something like Morning Bear, isn't it?" Jenny was confused. "You told me I was warm."

"You are, Jenny. You really are."

"Is it Borning Bear or Corning Bear or Dorning Bear or Forning Bear?" she tried.

"Sorry!" Mr Hoffman shook his head again.

"Oh, I'll never guess!" Jenny sighed. "I'll never get to take him home."

"Don't give up," he told her. "If you keep thinking and trying, I really believe you might get it right."

That night Jenny couldn't sleep. There were hundreds of names racing around in her head, but none of them seemed right — and then she realized why. Mr Hoffman had grown up in Germany, so his bear would have a German name!

The trouble was, Jenny didn't know any.

"Still awake, love?" Her mum came in

and sat on the bed. "I suppose you're excited about Christmas. I'm afraid it'll only be home-made presents again this year."

"That's all right, Mum," said Jenny. "I like home-made presents."

But she didn't tell her about the one she wanted most of all. What was the point? Morning Bear wasn't even for sale.

"Oh, if only Morgan was still here," said her mum, under her breath. "It's so hard without him…"

"My daddy, you mean?" asked Jenny.

Her mum nodded and hugged her tight. "I miss him so much," she whispered. "Especially at Christmas."

Jenny picked up the photograph of her father from beside the bed. He looked so tall and handsome in his smart uniform. She could hardly remember him, though, for he'd been a pilot in the war. The plane he'd been flying had disappeared when Jenny was only three, and he'd never returned.

"You called him Morgan just now, Mum," said Jenny quietly. "But I always thought his name was Taffy."

"Oh no, love." Her mother swallowed hard. "That's what everyone called him, because he came from Wales, but Morgan was his real name. I was the only one who used it, and only when we were alone together."

"Mum?" asked Jenny, after a bit. "What does Morgan mean?"

"I've no idea, love. I'm not sure it means

anything, really. Why?"

"Because Mr Hoffman, down at the junk shop, always says 'Gooten Morgan' to me on the way to school. He's not talking about my dad, is he?"

"Oh no!" Her mum laughed. "That's because he's from Germany. He came here before the war. *'Guten Morgen'* means 'good morning' in German. *'Guten'* is good, and *'Morgen'* is morning."

Jenny thought for a while. "So my dad was Morning Edwards, then?"

"I suppose so, in a funny sort of a way. He loved mornings, and greeted every new day with a smile."

In Jenny's dream, she was with her dad and the bear, flying high above the clouds.

And first thing in the morning she sat up in bed, wide awake, with a feeling that she just might know the answer to the most important question of all.

"*Guten Morgen*, Mr Hoffman!" said Jenny, bright and early for school. "*Guten Morgen*, Morgan Bear!"

Mr Hoffman stared at her. "What was that you said, Jenny?" he asked. "What did you call my bear?"

"Morgan," said Jenny. "Like my dad!"

She glanced at the shop window, and the lovely little bear seemed to be smiling back at her.

"You've got it, Jenny!" said Mr Hoffman,

his eyes wide in surprise. "For that's his name – *Morgen-Bär*. It's the German for Morning Bear. It's what I called him when I was a small boy, because he was always there by my bed when I woke up, waiting for me to jump up and play with him."

He hurried into the shop, reached into the window and picked up the little bear.

"*Auf Wiedersehen, Morgen-Bär*," he said, patting him fondly. "Goodbye, little bear."

He handed the teddy to Jenny. "Here you are," he said. "He's yours now. An early Christmas present."

"Really, Mr Hoffman? Oh, thank you!" She hugged the bear tight. "I'll love him every day of my life. But won't you miss him?"

"Yes, Jenny, I will. But I know he'll be happy, and I know he'll make you happy, too. Will you put him in your own front window sometimes, so he can still watch the world go by?"

"Oh yes," said Jenny. "Of course I will."

"And can I come and visit him?" asked the old shopkeeper.

"Come on Christmas Day, for breakfast!"
cried Jenny.

So on Christmas morning, there were
four round the table in Jenny's house. There
was her mum, at one end. Mr Hoffman sat
at the other end. On the third chair was
Jenny, with the biggest ever smile on her
face. And on the fourth chair was Morning
Bear – the newest, and smallest, member of
the family.

THE KITTEN IN
THE SNOW

Penny Dolan

The front door opened and a gust of wintry wind rushed into the house. Tilly put down her crayons and ran into the hall.

"Dad! Grandpa Joe!" she cried. "Did you get our kitten? Did you?"

A few weeks ago, before Christmas, Mum and Dad had taken Tilly and her big brother Ollie to the cat lady's house to see a litter of kittens. The kitten Tilly and Ollie chose looked like a tiny bundle of white fur.

"She's too young to leave her mother now," the lady had said. "I'll phone when it's time to collect her."

Yesterday evening, the lady had rung, and now Dad was carrying a cat basket carefully from the car. Tilly jumped up and down with happiness.

While Grandpa Joe shut the front door to keep out the cold, Dad took the basket into the living room. He placed it gently down on the floor.

"Please let me look," begged Tilly. "Ollie will be downstairs in a minute."

She peeped through the gaps in the basket. There was the small white kitten, fast asleep on a scrap of soft blanket.

"She'll wake up soon, Tilly," said Mum.

Tilly waited quietly and wondered what to call their new white kitten.

The kitten opened her eyes. She stretched herself, all the way from her pointed white ears to the tip of her tiny white tail. Then she peeped through the gaps in the cat basket and sniffed. Oh dear! This place didn't smell like home. The scrap of blanket was the only smell she knew. Wherever was she?

Outside the basket was a nice comfortable room, decorated all over with sparkly things and brightly coloured bits of paper. How odd!

Then she blinked in surprise. A tree was standing in the corner of the room! It did not look like any tree she had ever seen before. All the branches were covered in shiny balls and bright lights, and at the top was a beautiful winged angel.

Then the kitten saw a girl kneeling on the carpet nearby. The girl had a very smiley face.

"Come and look, Ollie!" Tilly called happily. "She's woken up at last."

Her brother smiled. "Wow, Tilly! She's so cute!"

"What name are you going to give her?" said Mum.

"We haven't thought of one yet," Tilly said, turning to her brother.

"We'll just call her Kitten for now," said Ollie, with a shrug.

The kitten liked Tilly's soft voice and the way Tilly left the door of the cat basket open so she could clamber out when she was ready.

She felt slightly scared by the grown-ups with their big feet and noisy voices, and by Grandpa Joe's loud laughter. Tilly tickled her gently just behind the ears, and soon she felt brave enough to make a funny little jump out into Tilly's lap.

"Hello, Kitten," said Tilly.

The kitten licked Tilly's hand with a rough pink tongue, and purred to show they were friends. Then she set off, exploring round the room.

She went to sniff round everybody's shoes, and then all around the furniture. She had just started nuzzling the fluffy rug when Dad sneezed so loudly that she hurried back to Tilly's lap.

But the kitten couldn't help being interested in everything, especially the strange tree in the corner of the room. Why was it there? It was not like the trees she'd seen through the window of her old home. Round, shiny balls hung from this tree's branches.

She could see kitten-faces hiding in some of the baubles and she patted one with her paw. *Tap! Tap! Ouch!* The bauble bounced back and rapped her on the nose. She hissed at the tree. How dare it try to hurt her? She scampered back to the safety of Tilly's lap. This was her place now!

That afternoon, Tilly and Ollie showed the small kitten all the rooms, upstairs and down. They showed her the cat bowl by the kitchen cupboard and the cat-litter tray over by the back door.

Ollie opened the back door wide. "There's our garden, Kitten," he said. "One day you'll be able to play out there."

Kitten looked out into the garden and sniffed. Her whiskers prickled. Her fur fluffed up all round her body. Outside smelt so very interesting! Kitten saw trees to climb up and overgrown plants to prowl through and great big bushes to scramble under. She took a deep breath, put one paw on the step and...

"Oh no, you don't!" said Mum, hurriedly picking up the little cat and carrying her back into the living room. "Kitten must stay indoors for now. For one thing, it's very cold out there. And for another, she needs to know the scent of her new home. If she doesn't, she could easily get lost."

"Oh, I almost forgot," said Ollie, reaching into a drawer. He brought out a new kitten collar with a tiny, jingling bell and handed it to Tilly. "I got this especially for her."

"Ollie, what a clever idea," Tilly said, 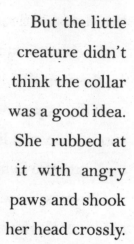 fastening the collar round the kitten's neck. But the little creature didn't think the collar was a good idea. She rubbed at it with angry paws and shook her head crossly.

"So when can Kitten go out?" asked Ollie.

"In about a week," Mum told them.

Gradually, through the day, the kitten got used to her collar, even though she found it hard to enjoy hide and seek when her jingling bell always told Tilly and

Ollie where she had gone.

"Oh dear! I still don't know what we should call her," Tilly said, as she stroked her sleepy little pet.

"Tiger? Fattypuss? Pussykins?" suggested Ollie.

Tilly shook her head. "No! None of those," she said, yawning.

The little kitten yawned too.

"Names can wait," said Mum. "Right now it looks like bedtime for all of you."

They showed the kitten her cosy new cat bed by the radiator in the kitchen. She sniffed to check it was really hers. Yes, her own blanket was tucked inside. So she stepped in, curled round once and fell asleep immediately.

Kitten woke to the sound of the birds singing outside. She could hear someone moving, too. She jumped out of her new bed, listening.

Grandpa Joe wandered downstairs in his pyjamas, humming along to the music on his earphones. Such big feet! The kitten darted behind the kitchen bin.

Grandpa Joe switched on the kettle for his morning mug of tea. He was so sleepy that he didn't even remember about the kitten. While the kettle boiled, he opened the back door. He gazed out at the long, wintry garden, taking big deep breaths.

So did the kitten. She could smell that

wonderful fresh air, too. Silently, she crept out on to the step behind him.

Grandpa Joe rubbed his eyes sleepily. Brrr! It was cold out there! Quickly he went in and closed the door, and took his tea back upstairs to bed.

Meow! Meow! the kitten called, but Joe didn't hear her. Nobody heard her. She was outside, all alone!

Even though she was a little bit afraid, she soon decided to go exploring. She tiptoed across the frosty grass. *Ouch!* The lawn felt hard and cold under her paws. The kitten fluffed her furry coat up warmly so she would feel bigger and braver.

The icy wind didn't think the kitten was any bigger. It blew so fiercely she felt as if she was being pushed along, jingling as she went. She scampered this way and that until she ended up in the shelter of an old bush, way down the long garden. She sat up and shook her whiskers. She was sure she was still in the same garden, but which was the way back?

She crept along a path until she came to the edge of a shallow icy pond. A gang of cheeky sparrows sat there, cheeping rudely and not one bit afraid.

She leaped at them, her bell jingling. Oh! The ice was so slippery under her white paws that she slid across into a clump of grass.

"Silly kitten! Silly kitten!" The sparrows flew off, twittering with laughter.

Meow! Meow! she called, as she clambered back to safety. She would not go on that horrid ice again!

Now dark grey clouds had filled the sky and tiny flakes of snow were tumbling down. It was so very cold! Kitten shivered. She was fed up with exploring now. Oh dear, where was her home?

All at once, a dark shape with reddish fur came hurrying into view. A fox! Kitten froze, scared to move in case she made the bell on her collar jingle.

The fox looked towards her. He showed his sharp, hungry teeth, and took one pace in her direction. At that very moment, the snow fell in a fierce flurry, faster and faster, thicker and thicker, as if the air was full of whirling white feathers. Even the keen-eyed fox could not see the small white kitten against the snow.

The fox waited, but then he turned as he heard someone down the street dropping rubbish into a dustbin. He grinned, revealing his sharp teeth. Then off he loped, with his tail all bushy behind him, hoping to find a better breakfast in the bin.

Kitten was glad that the fox had gone, but by now she was really cold. She felt too tired to move. The swirling snowflakes were wrapping her soft white fur under an icy blanket. She sniffed, but could find no scent of home at all.

Meow! she cried piteously.

She wished she hadn't gone out into the garden. Where were Tilly and Ollie? How would they ever find a white kitten in the snow? She crouched down and closed her eyes. She was lost, lost.

Then, from far down the other end of the long garden, she heard voices.

"Kitten? Kitten?" called Tilly.

"Where are you?" called Ollie.

The kitten tried to get out of the snowdrift. She yowled as loudly as she could, but the harsh wind had set the trees moaning so nobody could hear her.

Then she remembered the bell on her collar. This time she *needed* to be heard! Even though the kitten was so very tired, she shook the snow off her back and jingled her bell as loudly as she could.

The wild wind dropped for a moment. In the silence, Ollie and Tilly heard the silvery tinkling of the bell.

Suddenly, the children were there beside her.

"Oh, you poor thing!" Tilly said, scooping up the tired kitten and brushing the snow off her fur. "You're so cold!"

"We searched everywhere in the house," said Ollie. "We were afraid you'd run away."

Meow! the kitten cried, as Tilly carried her all the way home.

Tilly let the kitten snuggle sleepily in her lap. Just as Kitten closed her eyes, she heard Tilly's soft voice saying, "How about Snowflake? I think that would be a pretty name."

"Just perfect!" agreed Ollie.

The kitten purred contentedly, as if she was agreeing too. She was so happy to be back in her warm, safe new home.

TIGER IN
THE NIGHT

Narinder Dhami

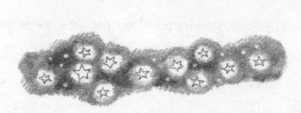

"It's my turn to sleep in the middle!" Rusty said with a little growl. He jumped on top of his brother and sister, and tried to wriggle his way in-between them.

"No, it's *my* turn," said Tiggy. She nipped Rusty's ear gently, just to show she wouldn't be pushed around.

"Let's fight for it!" Stripe suggested. He was the biggest of the cubs, so he enjoyed play-fighting because he usually won.

"It's time for little tigers all over the world to go to sleep," their mother said. She padded across the leafy floor of the den and scooped up Rusty by the scruff of his neck. She snuggled him down next to Tiggy, then did the same with Stripe.

"See?" said Tiggy, who was now sandwiched cosily between her two brothers. "I *told* you it was my turn!"

"Settle down now," Mum told them. "I'm going hunting for food, but you'll be warm and safe here in our den while I'm gone."

"You'll come back soon, won't you, Mum?" asked Rusty, curling his tail around himself.

"Of course I will," replied Mum. "And one day, when you're bigger, I'll take you with me and teach you all about being a Siberian tiger."

"We're special tigers, aren't we, Mum?" Tiggy asked. She couldn't wait to grow up to be as beautiful as their mother, with her thick orange fur and dark stripes. Their mum was very brave, too, Tiggy thought. Every night she went out into the cold and the dark to find them food.

"That's right," Mum agreed. "We're *very* special tigers because we live in one of the coldest places in the whole world."

Rusty gazed out of the cave. He could see a pale full moon hanging in the dark sky. The den was hidden in a forest of tall pine trees, and everything outside was cocooned in deep layers of pure-white snow. The snow had been there ever since the cubs were born, but their mother had told them that some day soon it would melt.

"Now, what do I always tell you before I go hunting?" Mum reminded them.

"Nighty-night, sleep tight and don't go outside or you'll get a fright!" the cubs chanted.

"Because there are nasty bears and wolves out there," added Stripe. During the daytime the cubs were allowed to play just outside the den while their mother watched over them. But when she went out at night, they had to stay indoors. Sometimes Stripe and the others heard wolves howling in the darkness. They sounded scary.

"Clever little cubs!" Mum licked each one lovingly. "When your dad visits us, he's going to be very proud of you."

"When will he come?" asked Tiggy eagerly. The cubs were still waiting to meet their dad for the first time.

"Before the snow melts," Mum replied. She went over to the entrance to the cave and slipped out into the moonlit forest. The cubs watched her until she disappeared from sight among the dark trees.

"I'm not sleepy yet," Rusty complained.

"Me neither," Tiggy said, sitting up. "Shall we play a game?"

"Oh, yes, let's!" Rusty agreed. "And if I win, then *I* get to sleep in the middle!"

"We could play the Dare Game," Stripe suggested.

"Good idea!" Rusty and Tiggy chorused. The Dare Game was one of their favourites, and they often played it when they were outside in the daylight. They dared each other to do all sorts of things, from rolling down slopes to climbing trees. If anyone refused a dare, they lost the game.

"Who's going first?" asked Stripe.

"Me, me!" Rusty bounced up and down excitedly. Secretly he'd just thought of something that would make the Dare Game a whole lot more exciting. "I've got some *great* dares!"

"No, me first!" Tiggy insisted. "You were first last time we played."

Rusty heaved a sigh. "OK," he agreed.

"This is for Stripe," Tiggy announced. "I dare you to eat some of these leaves." And she patted the leaf-strewn floor of the den with her paw.

Stripe groaned. "Tigers don't eat leaves!" he grumbled. But he picked up a few in his teeth and began to munch on them. The disgusted look on his face made Tiggy and Rusty laugh.

"They taste horrible!" Stripe growled, and he spat the leaves out.

"My turn! This dare is for Tiggy." Rusty gazed at his sister, his eyes shining with mischief. "I dare you to go outside the den!"

Tiggy could hardly believe her ears. "I can't, Rusty," she gasped. "You know we're not allowed."

"If you don't, you'll lose the game," Rusty pointed out. "And then I get to sleep in the middle!"

"He's got you, Tigs!" Stripe laughed.

Tiggy hesitated for a moment. None of them had ever dared go outside the den when their mother wasn't there. Mum would be *very* angry if she found out, Tiggy knew. But she couldn't turn down a dare, or her brothers would never let her forget it...

"All right," Tiggy said at last. "I'll walk twenty steps out of the den and back again!"

"Tiggy, wait!" Rusty cried. "I was only joking. Come back!"

But it was too late. Tiggy had already bounded outside into the black night.

Everything looked different to the daytime, Tiggy thought, shaking a little with fright. The cool, pale light of the moon wasn't warm and friendly like the sunshine, and there were dark shadows lurking everywhere. Tiggy waded through the snow, counting steps.

"Sixteen, seventeen, eighteen—"

Suddenly, Tiggy missed her footing. With a yelp, she fell, tumbling head over paws down a long slope. As she lay at the bottom, feeling dazed, she heard frantic shouts.

"TIGGY!" Stripe yelled. "Where are you?"

"I'm sorry, Tiggy," Rusty called. "Please come back!"

Tiggy struggled to stand upright. "I'm here!" she cried, shaking the snowflakes from her whiskers.

A moment later, Stripe and Rusty ran down the slope towards her. Rusty got stuck in a snowdrift, but Stripe grabbed him by the scruff of his neck and pulled him out.

"Are you all right, Tiggy?" asked Rusty. He licked a snowflake off her ear. "I'm sorry. I didn't *really* think you'd do the dare!"

"I shouldn't have," Tiggy admitted. "We'd better go home before Mum catches us!"

"What's that?" Stripe said, suddenly spotting a flash of silver across the snow. It was a small animal with big ears and a long, brush-like tail.

"It's a silver fox!" Rusty cried. "Let's chase him!"

He took off after the fox, and the others followed. It was great fun chasing the fox through the shadowy trees in the moonlight, Rusty thought gleefully. Much better than lying asleep in the den!

After a while, though, the fox ran off and vanished into a hole that was too small for the cubs to follow him down.

"Good night, Mr Fox!" Stripe called after him.

Tiggy was gazing nervously around

the forest. "Where *are* we?" she asked.

Stripe sniffed the air, trying to catch the scent of home. But he couldn't, and that frightened him. *You have to stay strong for the others because you're the biggest,* Stripe told himself. "We can't be that far from the den," he said.

"Let's follow our trail and retrace our steps," Tiggy suggested.

CRACK!

The loud noise of a twig snapping made the cubs jump in fright.

"Is anyone there?" Stripe called. He tried to growl menacingly, but it came out as a scared little yelp.

A big, dark shadow emerged silently from behind one of the trees. This animal looked lean and mean. He was covered in grey fur and had piercing yellow eyes. His gaze was fixed on the cubs and it didn't waver for an instant as he slunk towards them.

"I think it's a wolf!" Tiggy whispered, remembering what their mum had told them.

"We're just off home, Mr Wolf," Stripe said bravely. "Goodnight!"

The cubs turned to run, but the wolf had already sprung forward to stop them. Staring hungrily at Rusty, who was nearest, he began to close in on the little tiger cub.

"You leave my brother alone, you big bully!" Tiggy cried. She grabbed hold of the wolf's tail, clinging on for dear life. Stripe joined in too, snapping at the wolf's legs.

The wolf howled furiously, trying to shake Tiggy off, but she wouldn't let go.

"Run, Rusty!" shouted Stripe.

"I'm not leaving you and Tiggy," Rusty yelped.

The wolf snarled and took another step towards Rusty, looming over him.

All of a sudden, out of nowhere, a loud, bone-chilling growl echoed through the trees. The tiger cubs and the wolf froze to the spot.

GRRROWWWL!

There it was again. Then the three cubs and the wolf saw a magnificent, fully-grown tiger charging through the trees towards them at full speed. His tail was thrashing angrily and his golden-amber eyes were shining in the moonlight.

The wolf hesitated. He growled at the advancing tiger and for a moment he stood his ground. But as the tiger came closer, the wolf finally turned and slunk away.

The huge tiger stopped in front of the three cubs, and stared at them sternly.

The cubs huddled together nervously.

"Does your mother know you're outside at night?" he asked in a deep, growly voice.

The cubs looked very ashamed of themselves.

"No, sir," Stripe whispered.

"Then I shall take you safely back to your den," the tiger told them. "Follow me." He turned, but then glanced back at them. "And don't call me *sir*. You can call me *Dad*."

Stripe, Tiggy and Rusty stared at each other in amazement as the tiger strolled off.

"It's our dad!" Rusty muttered.

"Do you think he'll tell Mum?" asked Tiggy.

"We're in big trouble now," Stripe said with a sigh.

Gloomily, the three cubs followed their father back to the den.

"What does your mother say to you before she goes hunting?" asked Dad, as the cubs settled down on their bed of leaves.

"Nighty-night, sleep tight and don't go outside or you'll get a fright," Stripe said.

"And you *did* get a fright tonight, didn't you?" Dad reminded them.

The cubs looked miserable.

"You shouldn't have gone out, but you *were* very brave when you were fighting off that wolf," Dad told them. "I can see that you're going to be bold and beautiful Siberian tigers, and I'm very proud of you! I shall tell your mum that, too."

Rusty, Tiggy and Stripe couldn't believe their ears. "Thanks, Dad!" they gasped.

"Now go to sleep," said their father. "I shall keep watch until your mother comes home."

The three happy little tiger cubs snuggled down together with Tiggy in the middle. A few minutes later, they were fast asleep, dreaming of all the fun they were going to have tomorrow with their mum and dad.

JUST IN TIME FOR CHRISTMAS

Holly Webb

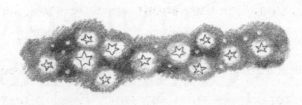

"I hate this time of year," one of the girls at the shelter sighed, as she opened the door on to the exercise run, and four excited dogs shot past her. They were barking so loudly they drowned out the carols on the radio in Reception.

"Christmas?" Her friend Lucy stared at her. "How can you hate Christmas, Kate? That's awful!"

"Not everything about Christmas..."

Kate stopped talking to glare at one of the dogs racing about outside, and he slunk away from the smaller dog he'd been squabbling with. "But when the shelter closes on Christmas Eve, it just makes me feel so sad, thinking of all the dogs shut in here on Christmas Day. I know they get a special lunch and extra treats, and I've bought them all some rawhide chews. But it isn't the same. They ought to be with a family for Christmas. Or anyone, really. A proper home of their own."

Lucy made a face. "Now you've got me all miserable, too." She sighed. "Well, we've got a few more days to find this lot the perfect home."

A little later, Max, the terrier-cross, came in from the run with his eyes sparkling. It was his favourite twenty minutes of the day.

The run was a big fenced-in area, where a few dogs could be let out at a time, so they had a chance to really stretch their legs. The dogs in the shelter didn't get a lot of exercise. There were a few volunteers who came and took them out for walks, but never enough, and there were lots of dogs in at the moment, and not very many people rehoming them. It was such a busy time of year – hardly anyone wanted to get a new dog just before Christmas.

Everyone at the shelter was hopeful about Max, though. He was so sweet – very young, not much more than a puppy, and he had short golden-brown fur, big soulful dark eyes, and enormous ears that looked like they were really meant for a dog a couple of sizes bigger than he was. And Max was friendly, too – so surely someone would want to take him home?

"You know, I thought you were going the other day," Kate murmured to Max a couple of days later, as she scratched his ears through the wire of his pen, and he leaned against it, his eyes blissfully closed. "That man really liked you. I suppose he did take Buster, and Buster had been here for ages. But I wish you could have a proper home before Christmas, Max."

Max gave her hand a lick. "It isn't likely to happen now, though," Kate added sadly. "It's Christmas Eve. We're open, but I don't know if we'll get anyone coming. Oh, there's the phone. Maybe someone wants to come and visit, after all." She dashed off to Reception to answer it.

Max yawned, and settled down in his basket for a sleep. He didn't mind the shelter as much as some of the dogs, who scratched and whined all the time. But he did wish they got more time to run about. His first home had been with an old lady, Mrs Jarrett, who'd got him for some company. She'd loved having him, but she wasn't really able to look after him properly, and so he'd ended up in the shelter.

He'd liked it best at his old home when Mrs Jarrett's grandchildren came round and played with him. His favourite was Maisie. He liked the boys, Josh and Jayden, as well, especially when they played football with him. But Maisie was so good at cuddling him, and scratching his ears and the itchy bit under his chin. He loved to snooze with his head in Maisie's lap. He wished he could see Maisie again. Every time he heard a girl's voice among the visitors to the shelter, he would look for her hopefully, but she never came to see him.

He buried his head under the cushion in his basket, and tried to remember how it felt when Maisie hugged him. He slept, his paws scrabbling every so often as he dreamed. Football. Chasing around Mrs Jarrett's garden. The children giggling as the ball went into a big patch of purple flowers, and they had to get it out quick before Mum or Gran noticed. He was dashing up and down the garden after them, barking at the ball. Then back into the house for a drink of water, and some of his favourite treats from the shiny bag in the cupboard. He could hear Maisie laughing as he gobbled them down, and he whined in his sleep, missing her all over again.

"Hey, Maxie…"

Max wriggled blissfully as the dream-Maisie stroked him, and called his name.

"Max!"

Max shook himself blearily, and pulled his head out from under the cushion. Was it food time again already? Or perhaps he was getting an extra walk? He looked up to see who was outside his pen.

Then he leaped out of his basket and threw himself at the side of the pen, barking and barking like a mad thing.

It hadn't been a dream! Or not all of it. Maisie really had been calling his name.

"Oh, Mum, look, he remembers us!" Maisie knelt down next to the wire pen, and Max licked her cheek lovingly.

"He really does." Her mum sounded surprised.

"I've missed you, Maxie," Maisie told him. "Mum says she's sick of me moping round the house."

"Crying all the time," Josh put in, as he tickled Max under the chin. "We've missed you too, Max."

"So if we take turns feeding you, and

walking you, and we promise to clear up any mess, Mum says we can take you home!" Maisie beamed at him.

Max looked back at her hopefully. He wasn't sure what she was saying, but from her voice, it seemed to be a good thing. Maybe she was going to take him for a walk?

Kate was smiling down at him, and she had a lead in her hand – his old lead, blue with pawprints on. He recognized it. Mrs Jarrett had given it to the shelter when she brought him in, with all his other things in case they needed them. Josh was holding his old basket and food bowls, too, Max realized, his ears pricking up.

Were they taking him back home?

"Bye, Max! Happy Christmas!" Kate hugged him, and she was crying and smiling at the same time. "I put your Christmas dog chews in your basket," she called after him, as he walked out of the shelter, with Maisie holding his lead, sniffing at the cold winter air.

"It might snow tonight," Jayden said, as they hurried through the streets.

Max was walking close to Maisie, not wanting to let her go. She nearly tripped over him a couple of times. "Do you think he's cold?" she asked her mum worriedly.

But her mum smiled. "No, I think he's just glad he's got you back. He's such a sweet little dog. You were right, Maisie. We should have taken him home with us before."

Maisie nodded. Mum had said it wasn't a good idea to visit him at the shelter, because it would make her sad. It was actually nicer than she'd imagined, but no dog could really like it there. "Nearly home," she whispered lovingly to Max.

Max looked around him curiously. This wasn't his old home. There were more trees in the road, and lights everywhere, sparkling and flashing and changing colour. The house they stopped at had little white lights wrapped around a tree in the front garden.

The front door opened, and Maisie's dad was there, grinning. "You got him! Wow, he's bigger. Hello, Max!"

"He won't get bigger than this, honestly," Maisie told him, and Dad hugged her.

"I'm not changing my mind, Maisie, don't panic. It's great to see him again."

Max stared around the hallway, his tail twitching just a little. The house smelled good. He followed the children as they trooped into the kitchen, and Josh put his basket down by the radiator, and his bowls next to it. Maisie took off his lead, and hung it on a hook by the back door, as though it had always belonged there.

Then she picked him up – she could only just manage, now he was bigger – and carried him into the living room to see the Christmas tree.

"Look, Max! Isn't it beautiful?" She nuzzled her cheek into his fur as he nosed one of the glittering decorations. "But not as beautiful as you. You're home, Max! And just in time for Christmas."

Have you read…

A Winter's Night

A Heart-warming Treasury of Animal Stories

The Little Bunny and other animal tales